NINJA!

ARREE CHUNG

Henry Holt and Company
NEW YORK

A ninja needs

a thick
ninja **stick**,

silent ninja
footwear,

sticky
ninja **gloves,**

an
unbreakable
ninja
rope,

and a
bouncy ninja
paddle.

A ninja **sneaks,**

When a ninja
finds his
target,

he must overcome obstacles.

He will face **danger**,

show **courage**,

and find the **strength** to defeat angry beasts.

A ninja

must
master

the
element
of . . .

to capture...

He must go into enemy territory,

scale walls,

remain undetected,

and find the sacred cup.

Against all odds,

he must
believe

in his ability

to rebound

and
overcome

all challenges.

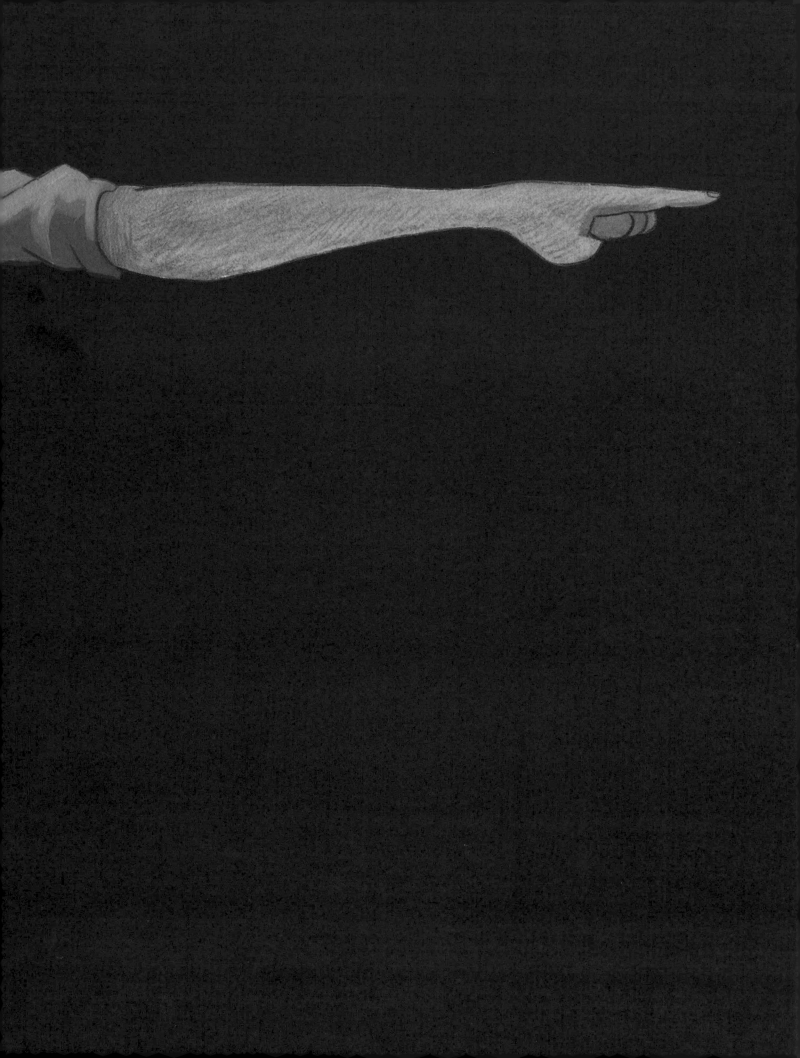

I am **dishonored.**

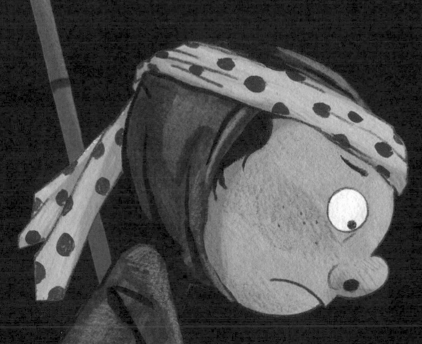

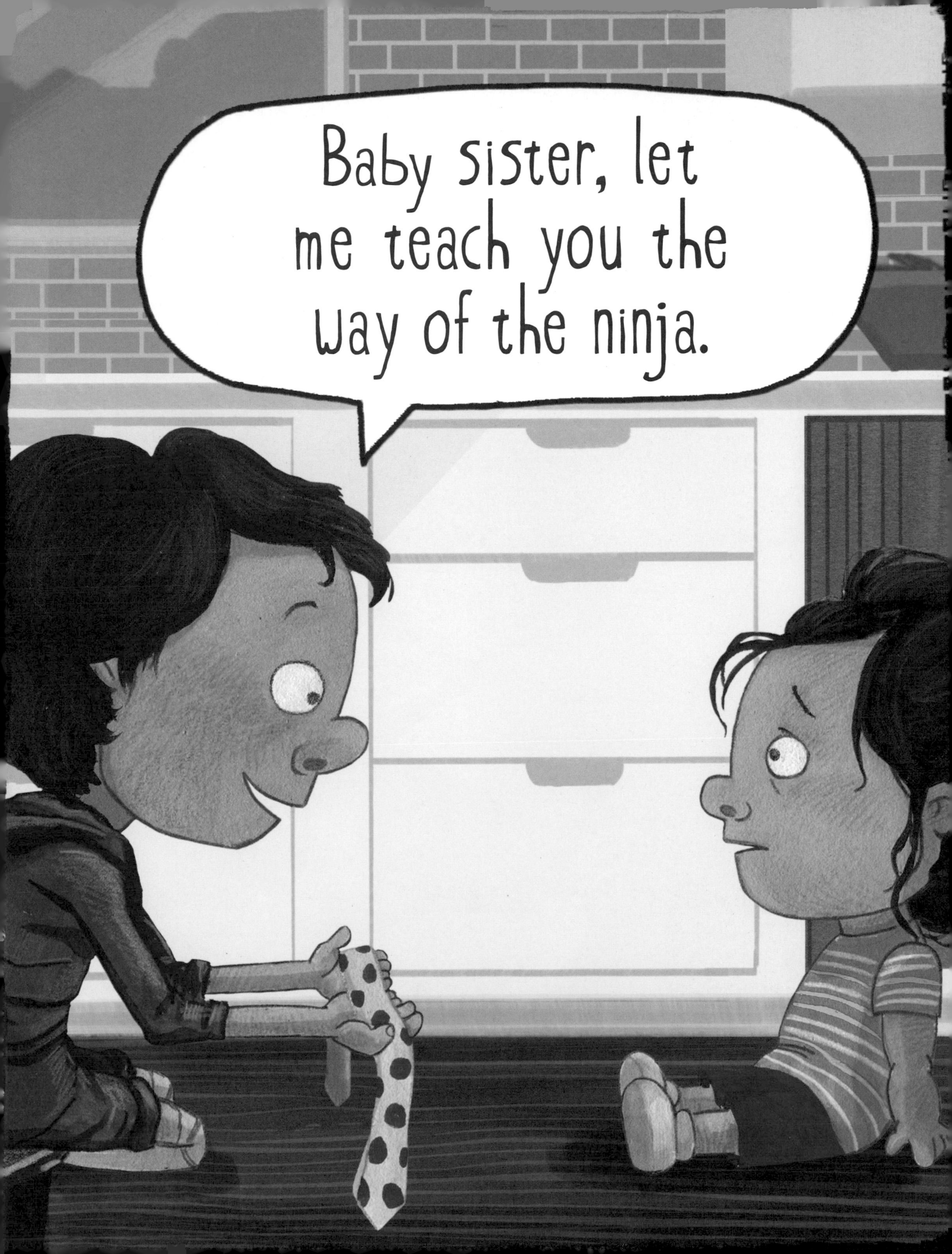
Baby sister, let me teach you the way of the ninja.

For Dad

Thank you, Rubin, Kate, and Laura, for believing in me,
and thank you to Mom, Art, Paul, Shelley, Nilesh, Lea,
Kevin, Jason, and Doug, for all the love and support.

Henry Holt and Company, LLC. *Publishers since 1866*
175 Fifth Avenue, New York, New York 10010
mackids.com

Henry Holt® is a registered trademark of Henry Holt and Company, LLC.
Copyright © 2014 by Arree Chung
All rights reserved.

Library of Congress Cataloging-in-Publication Data
Chung, Arree, author, illustrator.
Ninja! / Arree Chung. — First edition.
pages   cm
Summary: "A ninja must be strong, courageous, and silent! He creeps through the house on a secret mission.
There may be obstacles! But have no fear—a true ninja can overcome all challenges." —Provided by publisher
ISBN 978-0-8050-9911-9 (hardback)
[1. Ninja—Fiction. 2. Brothers and sisters—Fiction. 3. Play—Fiction.] I. Title.
PZ7.C4592Nin 2014   [E]—dc23   2013043353

Henry Holt books may be purchased for business or promotional use. For information
on bulk purchases, please contact Macmillan Corporate and Premium Sales Department
at (800) 221-7945 x5442 or by e-mail at specialmarkets@macmillan.com.

First Edition—2014 / Designed by Arree Chung and April Ward
Acrylic paint on Rives BFK paper, found paper, and Photoshop
were used to create the illustrations for this book.

Printed in China by Toppan Leefung Printing Ltd., Dongguan City, Guangdong Province

1 3 5 7 9 10 8 6 4 2